About the Author

David Melling was born in Oxford.
His first book was shortlisted for the Smarties
Book Award and The Kiss that Missed was
shortlisted for the Kate Greenaway Award.
He is married and lives with his wife
and children in Oxfordshire.

For more information, go to:
www.davidmelling.co.uk

Look
out for
all the
GOBLINS
books:

Stone Goblins
Tree Goblins
Puddle Goblins
Shadow Goblins

puddle GOBLINS

David Melling

h

*Hodder
Children's
Books*

A division of Hachette Children's Books

Text and illustrations copyright © 2008 David Melling

First published in Great Britain in 2008
by Hodder Children's Books

The right of David Melling to be identified as the Author and Illustrator
of the Work has been asserted by him in accordance with the
Copyright, Designs and Patents Act 1988.

I

A Catalogue record for this book is available from the British Library

ISBN-13: 978 0 340 94410 3

Printed and bound in Germany by GGP Media GmbH, Pößneck

The paper used in this book is a natural recyclable product made from
wood grown in sustainable forests. The hard coverboard is recycled.

Hodder Children's Books
A division of Hachette Children's Books
338 Euston Road, London NW1 3BH
An Hachette Livre UK Company

Fingerprints by Monika and Luka Melling

For Monika

who helped me pin down the little
details on our walks to school

MOODY STORM
(DOESN'T like goblins)

Goblin Hill

Bleak landscape

Bacterial Sponge
(Puddle Goblins Home)

puddles

GOOEY & GLOOP - smelly water goblins

(a big thank you to the slugs and snails who:

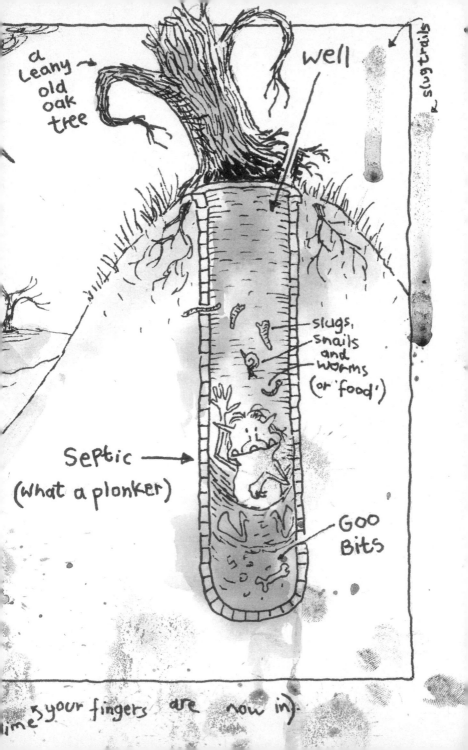

I'm sure you've heard of Water Goblins, even if you haven't seen them. But **Puddle** Goblins? These little tinkers have found a way to climb out of their watery holes and walk on dry land. How? With a puddle in their pants!

Of course, this drives your average Water Goblin bananas because they can't do this – everything needs to be wet whenever they go walking.

So what is the Puddle Goblin's secret?

I can't tell you that – it's a secret! Besides, if you dare tell a goblin secret they **will** find out.

They always do.

A few facts about Puddle Goblins

Habitat

Puddle Goblins live in *water holes* or *puddle-pits*. One puddle can fit one fat goblin, or a few smaller ones, as long as there's no fidgeting. A settlement of water holes is usually found in boggy marshlands, of much smelly honky-ness.

The characters in this book come from such a place, which they call *Bacterial Sponge* or *Home*!

Puddles

Puddle Goblins are so called because they have found ways of using puddles like no other creature.

 # Roll-ups

They can roll up puddles and carry them in their pocket, so they can walk on dry land. No one knows how they do this (that's the secret I was

telling you about), but

Water Goblins are

desperate to find out.

 # Puddling

If a Puddle Goblin is very nervous, it might lay down puddles every few metres or so. Some Puddle Goblins can enter one puddle and leave by another, anywhere along the line, and so avoid any danger. Once the goblin is inside, the puddle becomes sealed and soundproof. Nothing can reach it, and only the goblin that made the puddle can break the seal.

Note: If it is not used, a puddle will dry up just like any other puddle. But a puddle with a goblin inside will remain wet for as long as a goblin stays there. So if you come across a single puddle long after the rain has gone away, you'll know why.

Hunting and Frozen Puddles

Puddle Goblins like to hide in puddles on rainy days. A single finger from each hand, partly hidden by leaves, pokes out at the edges of a puddle. Fingers are very sensitive

and can detect the slightest vibration on the ground of anything passing by. If it's edible, they'll pounce! But on a cold winter day a puddle may freeze and a plonky goblin could find itself trapped until the ice melts.

(Some Puddle Goblins hunt in packs)

 # Water Goblins

Because they can't carry puddles and travel on dry land, Water Goblins are jealous of Puddle Goblins. They want, more than anything, to discover the secret of how to roll up, carry and climb into puddles. But meanwhile, they have come up with their own way of "travelling wet". Not with puddles, but with fish.

Fish-pants –
they can carry a fish in their pants.

Fish-fingers –
they can attach fish to their fingers.

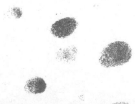 # A Giant's Toothpick

A Puddle Goblin's nightmare is to dry out!
A dried-out Puddle Goblin is as stiff as a stick,
and unable to move. Giants have been known to
use them as toothpicks. Nice.

INTRODUCING THE
PUDDLE GOBLINS
and friends

Bunion

Likes to think of himself as a leader. Doesn't like the word "Why".

Septic

Bit of a plonker for falling down a well, but quite relaxed about almost everything.

Tincup and Ribbit

Septic's friends at the bottom of the well – a moody bucket and an affectionate frog.

Teabag

A gentle giant of a Puddle Goblin. Not having a
waterproof head has caused him problems in the
brain department.

Fetid

Bunion's travel
buddy. Bit grumpy
and argumentative.

Knuckles

A finger-legged spider.
Most Puddle Goblins keep
one. They help unblock ears
and noses with their long
curly fingernails (don't ask).

Gooey and Gloop

Sister and brother. They are nasty and spiteful
Water Goblins who are always on the lookout
for Puddle Goblins to make them reveal their
folding-puddle secret.

THE CLOSE-UP BITS OF
A PUDDLE GOBLIN

*Hands – webbed hands
to help them swim.*

*Nose – often "rests" inside the
lower lip. This seals the nostrils,
making them waterproof.*

*Ears – Puddle
Goblins can
breathe
underwater,
through their
ears!*

Slugs and snails –
Puddle Goblins have
any number of them.
They're a bit of
company, and food!

Trousers or Puddle
Pants – large
balloon-sized trousers
can be filled up with
water. Also contain
waterweeds, slugs,
snails and even one
or two fish. Bit like
a mobile fish tank.
(Ready-made
puddles can also be
stored here – in case
of emergency.)

Contents

The Story Begins ...

One wet and soggy night, a lone figure was grunting his way up the steep bank of Goblin Hill. He sloshed noisily, because his pants were full of puddles! His name was Septic and he was a Puddle Goblin.

A strong wind began to whistle – not far away a storm was brewing.

At the top of the hill Septic noticed a curious shape, low down in the grass. It was under an old oak tree, broken and leaning at a sharp angle.

There were only two branches that curled downwards like arms, as if pointing.

He made his way towards it, and was surprised to see an old stone well looking up at him from the tangle of roots. Even so, it was barely visible, hidden by a thick scarf of twisted ivy. Septic climbed down into the space where the oak tree had stood tall and proud for so many years, and took a closer look.

The well was so old that the name given to it had long since melted with time, sinking deep down into the hillside where it lay among the bones of the Stone Goblins that built it.

Septic sniffed around it curiously, pulling at the ivy to get a better look. The well tried not to notice. It wasn't used to such attention and felt quite put out by all the tugging.

Septic peered in. There wasn't much to see –
just a big black hole. Picking up a small stone, he
held out his arm and dropped it in. He waited to
hear it land, but the longer he waited the more
nothing happened.

He tried again, a bigger stone this time. Then
he climbed up on to the ledge and leaned over.
Right over – you know, to give himself the best
chance of … *oops!*

He slipped.

There was nothing to hold on to but a fog of
darkness. Septic had been thinking the well
looked like an open mouth, and now that he was
falling down it he felt for all the world as if he

4

was being swallowed – the hot stale breath, the wet slimy walls and oh my, the falling!

He closed his eyes, expecting the worst, but when he did eventually land it was soft, warm and gooey!

A small collection of leggy insects gathered around the top of the well, listening curiously to a small miserable voice which had taken a full five minutes to come back up out of the darkness …

"Oh, *wingle-bats!*"

Rumbling Skies

The storm was feeling very pleased with itself. Wet and windy in all the right places, it had just spotted a second Puddle Goblin walking up the same hill. And this time the storm was right overhead – perfectly placed to dump some of its rain.

Bunion didn't mind – the rain drew out all the snails and slugs. He picked them up greedily and stuffed the lot down his trousers,

6

where he already had: three puddles, a family of newts, thirteen frogs, a fat toad, and more worms than he could possibly eat for tea. He giggled, enjoying the way they all wriggled and oozed around inside.

He was humming a happy tune and cheerfully making his way along the ridge when he heard a scream. Nothing too odd about that – there were plenty of reasons to scream if you weren't very good at hiding and you had that "eat me" look about you. No, this scream was different. It sounded like a Puddle Goblin, although Bunion couldn't be sure with the rain lashing down. Still, better go and check it out. He sniffed the air until he found it, still hanging in the wind. Screams always smelled funny, peppermint mainly.

The sudden and unexpected arrival of a storm, the first proper rain in weeks, meant that Water Goblins were *bound* to be on the prowl. It was no time to be a Puddle Goblin, out on a night like this … alone.

Not far away, fat drops of rain were bringing to life a small water hole close to a stream. Two Water Goblins, brother and sister, slowly emerged and scrambled up Goblin Hill to see what mischief they could make! Their names were Gooey and Gloop. They soon found an old well peeping out from under an oak tree, wriggled in amongst the roots and settled down to wait and see what might come their way.

Ambush Set

Gooey and Gloop didn't have long to wait.
Their sharp goblin eyes caught sight of a
movement on the horizon. From that distance it
looked like a black smudge on grey paper, so
heavy was the rain, but with squeals of delight
they soon realised it was a Puddle Goblin – and
it was coming straight towards them!

Their wet skin glistened and their long thin tongues, blue and cold, flickered in and out, tasting the air.

"Yes-sss, it'sss coming this-sss way, so it is-sss!" hissed Gloop. He was a fat goblin with warts the size of peas.

"Let'sss jump and pinch and scratch its-sss sss-silly trousers-sss, oh brother of mine!" said Gooey. No warts on her, but a smell that made strong trees shiver.

They snorted, and hissed, and slapped each other crossly for making too much noise.

Ever since Puddle Goblins had been able to walk on dry land, Water Goblins had been trying to find out how they did it. What was their secret? And now, at last, the answer could be walking straight towards Gooey and Gloop – just right for the pinching! Meanwhile, at the bottom of the well, Septic was a little bewildered but otherwise all right. There was no light at all, so he patted himself all over to check that all his important bits were still in the right place. Groping around himself, he found that he was sitting waist-deep in mud. He licked a bit off his finger. It tasted of boiled cabbage. He shrugged – it wasn't all bad, then.

Septic looked up, hoping to see the well's opening, but it was still night – complete darkness.

There was no way of knowing just how deep the well was, but it was deep enough because unfortunately, like all Puddle Goblins, he was not a good climber.

He thought about calling out. Perhaps someone would hear him. But then again, the someone might be a some*thing* … a snootle-pig, perhaps, or a wonky-beaked eagle. He didn't think either of them would jump down after him, but the very thought made the mud bubble around him.

"No Septic, me ol' wingle-bat, the trick is not to panic," he said to himself. "Nice and quiet."

"*Right!*" He blinked.

"Sit tight!" He sniffed.

"OK then." He blinked again.

"Absolutely …"

12

He sat, quietly fidgeting, for almost a minute. Then …

"HEEEEEEEEELLLLP!!"

But the rain was so heavy his cries were washed back down again, like water down a drain, before they even reached the top.

Bunion Runs into Trouble

Bunion stopped suddenly. There was that scream again – and it was definitely a Puddle Goblin.

The storm was all around him, loud and out of tune. He squinted, searching the skyline, and picked out a single tree, bent and out of shape. Something was wrong. His senses were alert now, but the wind and rain were stirring them all up and he could see and hear very little, and smell practically nothing. He understood now why Water Goblins liked this weather so much – it made them impossible to detect, almost invisible!

"Sssh! … hisss! … ow!"

More sounds. A rush of wind, or was it …
whispering? Just my imagination, thought
Bunion.

"*Ssshhh! Or it'll hear us-sss!*"

There it was again! Voices, surely. Sneaky.
Close by. He didn't like this at all.

"Who's there?" he shouted, taking a step
back.

The next thing he knew there were squeals all
around him – Water Goblins jumping and
hissing in the rain – dozens of them, or so it
seemed.

"Catch it, scratch it, make it sss-scream!"

"Yes-sss, yes-sss, yes-sss – what *fun*!"

Bunion stumbled, the two Water Goblins
hanging on to him. They wriggled and grabbled
at his clothes, and eventually he lost his balance.

But the Water Goblins didn't stop pinching,
scratching and slapping. And the hissing! They
sounded like angry snakes.

He felt long greedy fingers probing inside his
pockets, up his trouser legs, inside his ears –
more pinching and pulling.

"Get off me puddles!" snarled Bunion.

They were smaller than he was, but they were strong. There was always one hand or one foot holding on. Fastened to him. Sticking! *Squeezing!* It was like wrestling an octopus.

But somehow he managed to take out one of the puddles from his pocket and dropped it in front of him. Despite the rain, he could see exactly where it lay, and the Water Goblins were too busy to notice.

"Get *off* me!" he roared, angry now.

With an almighty effort, Bunion grabbed a handful of ears and twisted! The goblin screams drowned out the thunder for a moment.

And that moment was enough. Bunion jumped into the puddle.

Instantly, the puddle was sealed and the noises cut off. Bunion hung there, floating in a silent bubble of water just below the surface. Tiny bubbles clung to his hair and all around him. In slow motion he turned, still and calm, and looked up at the two angry faces, their soundless mouths spitting out curses, their fists pounding the puddle from above.

Bunion watched the Water Goblins, but they couldn't see him, only reflections of themselves. He knew he was safe. No other creature, not even another Puddle Goblin, can break the seal and climb into a puddle once it is full! Gooey and Gloop paced in circles around the puddle, furious that they couldn't get at him.

A Hiss Goodbye

Eventually Gooey and Gloop moved away from Bunion's puddle. He couldn't hear what they were saying, but they looked excited about something.

Suddenly the Water Goblins blocked out the sky. They had appeared suddenly, kneeling on top of the puddle, so close Bunion could see their green gummy eyes glistening with glee! They each held a stick, and set to work scraping and tearing at the puddle edges in an effort to tear it free and reach Bunion.

His best chance was to hope it would stop raining soon and then wait for the ground to dry, forcing the goblins back to their water holes. But this would take time, and judging by the storm's growling, it wasn't going to happen soon.

Bunion sighed. There was nothing he could do but wait.

The storm had really enjoyed itself. Such fun! But it was running out of rain now and it was time to leave. The storm looked around for something to hit with its last fork of lightning, and saw two prancing Water Goblins waving a stick – just the job.

Gooey and Gloop were holding hands and kicking clogs of mud up in the air. They were hissing, laughing and squealing, so sure were they of getting to the *"sss-sneaky toad hiding in puddle-sss!"*

And then the lightning struck. It hit Gooey right on her bonce and passed through her hand to Gloop!

The last spots of rain hit their hot frazzled
bodies, causing thin wisps of steam to hissssss.
It sounded very much like the hissing of Gooey
and Gloop, if only they could still hiss …

Chapter Five

Quiet at Last

Fortunately, the storm had given way to a warm sunny day, so by late afternoon Bunion could tell it was dry enough to come out. He touched the seal, which instantly melted, climbed out, rolled up the puddle and tucked it under his arm. He ran past the two black figures of Gooey and Gloop, still scorched to the spot.

"That should teach you plonks a lesson," he sniffed. Then he set off back home. Stiff as sticks, the Water Goblins could only blink at him, but their sharp eyes burned hatred.

Bunion knew he had been lucky. He wondered what had happened to the goblin he'd heard screaming. There were no screams now the storm had gone, just an eerie silence that hung in the air like a bad smell.

Septic had been shouting for help most of the night, but his cries had been smothered by the storm. He could do little now but *croak*, a sound that a resident frog mistook for a "hello". In one sloppy hop she joined Septic and gave his ankle a hug. She had been all alone in the well for a week now and any ankle was worth a hug, no matter who it belonged to.

Septic smiled. "Don't worry, my warty little friend, we'll be out of here in no time."

Six Months Later

Since the Water-Goblin attack, Bunion had been a little more cautious about travelling alone. Now he carried plenty of puddles with him, stuffed down the front of his trousers. That way, if he was attacked again he could set out a line of puddles that would create an escape route, and so avoid being trapped like last time.

Walking, however, was a problem.

His new *special* trousers were thirteen sizes too big. Now, he was more like a walking pond, but he had two friends to help him out. There was Fetid, a small Puddle Goblin with a temper squeezed into every part of his soggy warts.

It was his job to balance the front of the trousers on his head, shoulders and back – something he didn't really mind (though he often complained), because he got to eat anything that came out the bottom of Bunion's trouser legs.

And then there was Teabag. Everyone liked Teabag: he was a huge simple-minded goblin, heavy and very strong, and a useful friend to have if trouble came a-knocking. But it was always best not to confuse him with difficult questions. "Hello, Teabag, how are you?" was likely to be met with an expression that suggested he was shooing away imaginary flies with his eyebrows.

You see, Teabag's head wasn't waterproof. This was unusual for a Puddle Goblin and because of the amount of time he had spent in and around water over the years, things had got, well – *rinsed out*. Blinking, for Teabag, was a challenge.

It was six months since Septic's little accident and few goblins had passed the well in that time. But on this bright sunny morning Bunion and Fetid had bumped into Teabag, and together they decided to climb Goblin Hill.

When they reached the top, Bunion found the oak tree and the well pretty much as he remembered them.

They cleared a space around the rim of the well and sat down to play with their pets.

"Oi, who's trod on my newt?" groaned Fetid.

"How do you know someone trod on it?" said Bunion, feeling in his pocket for Knuckles, his finger-legged spider.

"Cos it's got a footprint on its head, that's how!"

"Not me," said Teabag, "I don't tread on nothing, me. In case they get too flat. Pets don't like being flat," he added.

"Don't look at me!" said Bunion.

"Well, *someone* did it," snapped Fetid.

"Maybe it did it itself," offered Teabag. "My Stoney's always having accidents."

Bunion and Fetid looked at each other.

"We told you, Teabag, Stoney isn't a pet, it's a stone," said Bunion.

Teabag frowned. He rummaged in his pocket and pulled out a small polished stone. "Don't listen to them, Stoney, they're only jealous cos their pets can't do tricks."

"What tricks?" asked Fetid.

"*Fetch*, and stuff!" Teabag sat up and smiled proudly. "I trained him all by myself."

"Go on then, show us," said Fetid, rolling his eyes.

Teabag tossed Stoney lightly in his hand, then threw it into the grass.

"What's it gonna fetch?" asked Bunion.

It was Teabag's turn to roll his eyes. "Well, we're not gonna know that till he comes back with something, are we?"

They waited.

Fetid cleared out a nostril.

"Yeah, now what?" said Bunion.

"He'll be back in a minute, you'll see."

Bunion and Fetid looked at each other again and smiled. The faint *ribbit* of a frog broke the silence.

Teabag stood up. "Stoney – is that you?" He grinned, his eyes widening. "Stoney can do frog impressions now – beat *that*!"

"What a plonker!" said Fetid, shaking his
head. But Bunion wasn't listening.

"Where did that frog noise come from?"
he asked.

"Down this here well, I think," said Fetid,
pointing over his shoulder.

Bunion turned round and examined the well
more closely.

"How many frogs you reckon are down
there?" he asked.

"How should I know?" said Fetid.

Bunion turned to Teabag, but he was wading
in the long grass calling out to his stone.

"C'mon, Stoney! Here boy, who's a clever
stone then, making frog noises. C'mon now,
come to Teabag!"

Bunion and Fetid decided to throw something down the well to see how deep it was.

"Where's my newt?" said Fetid quickly, just as Bunion dropped something familiar over the rim of the well.

"Dunno," said Bunion.

They both looked down the well and paused for a moment.

"*Did* you throw my newt down there, cos if you did I'll—"

Fetid stopped suddenly. A voice was coming up from the well! The two goblins gawped at each other. It was a quiet voice, but clear enough to understand …

"Ow!" it said. "That *hurt*. Right on me noggin!"

Septic

Septic had been down the well for a long time when Bunion and friends finally made their walk up Goblin Hill. He was keeping himself busy talking to a ground-bat.

"The first week was the worst. Definitely," said Septic. "Lonely. And dark. And no one to talk to. And dark. And lonely." He sniffed. "After that, well, it's just a bit samey I suppose, but not bad. There's sitting and thinking. And standing and thinking. And leaning against the wall and thinking. So you see, it's not *all* bad!"

Two tiny berry-black eyes pointed in the direction of Septic's voice. Like all ground-bats, he was almost blind. A little bewildered, he sat in Septic's lap and wondered why he hadn't been eaten yet. He tried to look as invisible and as *not there* as possible.

Septic's eyesight had weakened since he'd been in the well, sitting in a darkness that changed little throughout the day, and in a place so small he could touch the sides by holding out his arms.

He smiled and patted the ground-bat on the head. "Well, thanks for *dropping in!*" He giggled at his own joke, but stopped when he heard a *ribbit* sound coming from an upside-down bucket.

"Oh my, how *rude* of me!" said Septic. The bucket, now dented and rusty, had once dangled proudly from a strong and sturdy rope. Septic beamed. "I almost forgot my dear friends."

He stood up stiffly and held the frog in one hand, the bucket in the other. "This here is Ribbit, my chatty companion, and over here is Tincup. He doesn't like to say much. They're both long-term residents here in Well's Bottom." Septic giggled again, and the frog croaked. "I'm so sorry," he said, turning to the ground-bat, "I don't know your name, um, Mr …?"

The ground-bat blinked.

Septic smiled encouragingly.

"Ribbit," said Ribbit.

Tincup was quiet. Septic was right – he was a bucket of few words.

The ground-bat blinked
again.

"Well, perhaps we'll
meet again one day," said
Septic. In one slow
movement he flung the
ground-bat into the air. "Go
now, my fuzzy little friend.
Fly high and follow the light
at the end of the tunnel!"

Septic sat down and
crossed his legs.
Seconds later,
the flightless
ground-bat plopped
back down on to his
lap again.

"Oh, hello! *Another* fuzzy little bat – how nice of you to join me! I've just been talking to one of your funny friends. Have you been sent down to hear my fascinating story?"

The ground-bat was beginning to feel sick. He wondered why this Puddle Goblin kept throwing him up into the air.

"The first week was the worst. Definitely," said Septic. "Lonely. And dark. And no one to talk to. And …"

Septic and the ground-bat had been together like this for three days now. Septic had learned, over the months, to make the most of every visitor. And for those long, long gaps between visits, he had Ribbit and Tincup. But it was a struggle, at times, to keep cheerful, and the strain was beginning to show.

Just then a large flat newt bounced off his head.

"Ow!" he said. "That *hurt*. Right on me noggin!"

Chapter Eight

Is Anybody There?

Bunion, Fetid and Teabag were trying to make out what creature would possibly choose to live down a well.

"Hallooo! Anybody down there?" they called.

When Septic was first trapped down the well, he would spend a few hours a day calling for help. But as the days turned into weeks and then months he called less and less, until finally he gave up altogether. He spoke more quietly, whispering to himself and his companions. He started to mimic their speech, replacing words with croaks, gulps and burps, and a series of elaborate facial expressions And now, suddenly, a voice was calling down to him. He strained his head up, opened his mouth … "Ribbit?"

He cleared his throat and tried again.

"Hell-roak! *Ribbit!* Er … croak! … um, hello up there! *Ribbit!*"

Bunion, Fetid and Teabag couldn't work it out. It sounded like some poor goblin was being eaten by a giant frog.

They called out again, long and loud – trying to find out the goblin's name and how long he had been down there. But all they got in return were more croaks and *ribbits* mixed in with a selection of words that made little sense.

But they were convinced that whoever was down there seemed very keen on the idea of getting out.

It was Bunion's idea to go back down the hill to a stream lined with weeping willows. Here they could make a rope of some kind and pull this poor frog-goblin creature to safety.

"Last one back has smelly ears," said Teabag, who liked to turn everything into a game.

They raced off.

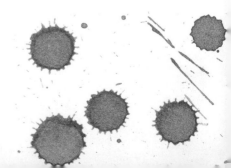

A Green-Eyed Spy

It had taken two days for Gooey and Gloop to free themselves from their crusty coats of charcoal. But the *zapped-with-lightning* experience had not gone to waste! At last they had seen how a Puddle Goblin uses a puddle. They had seen how Bunion took a puddle from inside his baggy nic-nacs, how he escaped by hiding *inside* the puddle, and then later, how he climbed out, rolled it up, and walked away! They didn't know how it was done, but it was a start.

They had every intention of stealing a puddle and finding out its secret as soon as possible. But for now, they realised that if they carried something wet, maybe, they too would be able to walk on dry land! Hmmm, a wet object. But what?

The answer, after much thought, was fish!

Water Goblins don't much care what they look like, so stuffing fish down their trousers was fine. And smelling of fish? Well, that was just lucky.

Now Gooey and Gloop were determined to hunt down Bunion and wreak a terrible revenge.

So it was that one fateful evening, about six months after being struck by lightning, Gooey was delighted to come across three Puddle Goblins, talking to a well. The curious thing was that the well appeared to be talking back to them!

"How interesting," she hissed quietly, smiling a long, thin smile – the type that made toothless ogres rock themselves to sleep at night. She set about weaving her weaselly way closer to the Puddle Goblins and their secrets.

"What-sss down that there hole then?" Her mouth curled at the edges and her blue tongue flashed.

Gooey's shining eyes watched them as they passed close to where she was hiding.

She listened to them twittering on about ropes
and rescue and tree branches. She waited some
time, making sure they had gone, then crawled
up to the lip of the well and rocked gently, eyes
closed, nostrils quivering.

She remembered this was the place where she
and her brother Gloop had been tricked by
that sneaky Puddle Goblin. She snarled at

the memory. At the time she had not
given the well much thought
but she took a closer look now.
She wasn't sure what the hole

was for, or why the Puddle Goblins were so
interested in it – perhaps there was something
down there?

Her tongue drew a wet sticky line along
her lips.

"I think-sss I shall need sss-some help with this-sss. Oh brother of mine, where are you?" She slid away from the well and into the grass.

A single wet handprint on dry stone was the only sign that a Water Goblin had been there – but that too disappeared in the warm breeze.

Septic could hear words floating down to him, but he wasn't sure if they were real or imagined. They were whispers of sound that made little sense. It was very confusing.

Could it be true? Had someone called out to him after all this time? Was he coming out of the well at last? The ground-bat had disappeared, so he hugged Tincup, and gave Ribbit a fond squeeze. "We might just be going home," he said. "We should pack! *Ribbit.*"

"Ribbit," said Ribbit.

The bucket was silent, deep in thought.

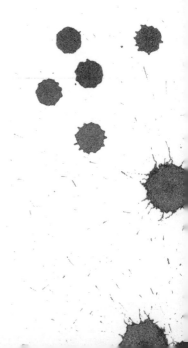

The Rescue Party ...
and More Trouble

Bunion was nervously chewing the nails of his pet spider, Knuckles. As Team Leader of the Rescue Party he felt he should be more in control.

Bunion, Fetid and Teabag had torn long strips of bark from the willows and were doing their best to twist and bend them into some sort of *laddery-rope-shape-type-thing*, as Bunion put it.

"Is that OK?" asked Teabag, holding up a piece between thumb and forefinger. It didn't touch the ground.

"Just a bit more – *you plonk*," said Bunion.

Fetid was busy with his strip, mumbling at the unfairness of it all. He wanted to be Team Leader, but Bunion had beaten him to it so he decided to sulk instead.

Finally, however, and much to everyone's surprise, they made something that looked like a rope, and Bunion led the way back to the well.

They passed a thicket of brambles that twitched and quivered with excitement, but they didn't notice it.

"Nice one, Gooey!" whispered Gloop.
Gooey had managed to drag her brother back
to the well. When he saw Bunion he let out
such a long hiss of satisfaction, it sounded like a
balloon with a slow puncture. He fiddled with
his warts – it helped him think. "That-sss him
all right – the sss-sneaky toad what hides in
puddle-sss!" His eyes flashed like steel knives as
Bunion hobbled past.

"And the smell?" asked Gooey.

"Hmm, I can smell sss-something down that
hole, as sure as frogs-legs is frogs-legs." He
drummed his fish-fingers impatiently. Gloop
found fish-pants uncomfortable and so had
taken to plugging one small fish on each of
his fingers.

"You did well coming to me, sss-sister.

We'll sss-sazzle his insides, we'll suck out his juices-sss, we'll …"

"Not sss-so fast," hissed Gooey. "We need-sss to find out what they're doing – and who are they talking to down that hole? It must be some kind of sss-secret to do with the puddles-sss they carry around, no? *Then* we'll—"

Before she could finish, a full set of fish-fingers slapped her across the mouth!

"Sssh! They're saying sss-something!"

Without another word they sank back into the brambles, silent as snails, and waited.

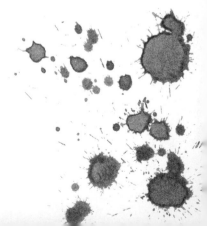

Is Anybody Down There?

The three Puddle Goblins approached the
well quietly. They were hoping to chance
upon something, a conversation, perhaps, a
song – anything that might tell them who was
down there.

They were delighted to hear that indeed,
someone was talking, ever so quietly. They
huddled around the well and listened carefully.

"Yes, I think you're right, Tincup. Ribbit can travel with
you, but make sure you have plenty of mud, Ribbit! He's
been down here longer than me and it'll be a bit of a shock,
is my guess."

There was a pause.

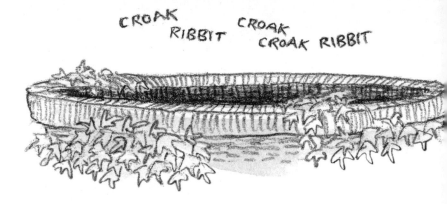

"Ribbit!" said the frog. "Ribbit, croak, ribbit."

"Now, now, my warty friend," came the same voice. "Don't worry about a thing, old Septic will look after you, Ribbit!"

Bunion, Fetid and Teabag looked at each other with open mouths. *Septic!* They were dimly aware of a story about a small Puddle Goblin who had gone missing during a storm. But that was *months* ago! Of course, Bunion quickly joined the dots. He jumped to his feet and called out.

"Septic? Septic? Are you down there, me ol' plonker?"

They all three strained to hear, excited that they had found the missing Puddle Goblin. There was no reply, so they tried again. And again. After five minutes they sat down, hoarse.

"I don't think he's in any more," said Teabag. "Shall we come back later?"

Way below, at the bottom of the well, Septic was trying to spoon out a little memory from his toffee-yoghurt brain.

Septic. That sounded familiar. After a slow, slow minute there was a flicker of recognition. Now that he thought about it … of course, it was *him.* He had been calling himself "Septic" all this time but somehow he'd forgotten it was his name!

Bunion stood up and tried again. "*Septic –* can you hear me?"

Again the Puddle Goblins held their breath, hoping to hear something.

"His voice is probably weak after all this time," said Fetid.

"Don't speak if it hurts," called Teabag with sympathy. "Just nod if you can hear us."

"I think," said Bunion, puffing out his chest dramatically, "we should get out … *The List!*"

The List

T he List was Bunion's plan of action. They'd
put it together right after Teabag had
suddenly, and quite unexpectedly, eaten one of
the ropes they had made earlier.

"You can't blame me," Teabag had groaned,
his tummy gurgling. "I haven't eaten anything
since the last time I ate something, and even then
it was …" He frowned and started again. "What
I mean is …"

So they had written The List. And now they
knew it was Septic down the well, they were
keen to get on with the rescue.

Bunion coughed. He took out a small piece of

paper. When he was sure he had the others'
attention he said, in a loud voice: "Number
One: Rocks!"

There was a flurry of activity. The goblins
picked up two rocks each, lined up and
threw them down the well.
Then they slipped their
hands in their pockets
and hung around,
drawing circles with
their feet in
the dirt.

"Er, I got a
question," said Fetid
suddenly.

"Well?" said Bunion.

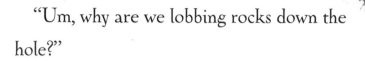

"Um, why are we lobbing rocks down the hole?"

Bunion rolled his eyes. "So Septic can pile them up, one on top of the other, and use them like a ladder to climb out." He didn't like being questioned. The rocks were his idea – top of The List!

"Ah."

"That's right clever, that is," agreed Teabag, nodding approval.

They fell silent.

"Hang about," said Fetid again. "If Septic doesn't know the rocks are coming down, some of them might squash him a bit – don't you reckon?"

Bunion's eyes widened. "Good point!" he said quickly.

As one, the three goblins shouted words of warning to Septic, suggesting he might want to look out for a pile of rocks that were on their way down and perhaps move out of the way!

There followed a complete and utter silence.

"A 'thank you' would have been nice," grumbled Fetid.

From the deep dark shadows, Septic continued to say nothing.

"Course," sniffed Fetid, "that's only six rocks he's got down there. I reckon he might need a few more, like."

"Yes, well, that's possible," said Bunion through gritted teeth. "But my rock was jolly big and I think you might be pleasantly surprised. He'll be popping his little head up any minute now – just you see."

More waiting.

"P'raps he's busy. You know, doing something else," suggested Teabag.

Bunion leaned over and gave him a pinch.

"Plonk!"

"Ow!"

"I was only wondering why he wasn't saying nothing, that's all – oooh, that *really* hurt ..."

"*I'm* finking them rocks weren't such a good idea," said Fetid.

"Why ever not?" snapped Bunion, feeling that his leadership was being given a bit of a prod.

"Well ... wouldn't it hurt? I mean, a pile of rocks landing on your nut – bound to hurt, that is!"

"Not if you catch them properly," insisted Bunion, folding his arms.

"I'm finking Fets is right," said Teabag. "Once I had a conker bounce off my head and I had a really big bruise. I bruise easy, me. All purple it was – and oooh, they don't half throb those bruises ..."

Bunion closed his eyes gloomily. He wondered if it counted being Team Leader if the team was full of plonks no brighter than a glow-worm's mud bath. He felt something move in his pocket and realised it was Knuckles. Gratefully, he pulled her out and started to chew her nails.

Septic had kept very quiet when he heard the voices from above. He really wasn't sure what to make of it all. When the rocks came tumbling down he was quite taken aback, but by some incredible fluke they all missed him. I suppose after six months trapped down a dark hole he was due a bit of luck!

The Puddle Goblins worked their way down The List. Fetid and Teabag wrote down one idea each whilst Bunion had added two and one for luck because he was leader.

He was quite put out by the rock idea not working. With a sigh he took another look at The List:

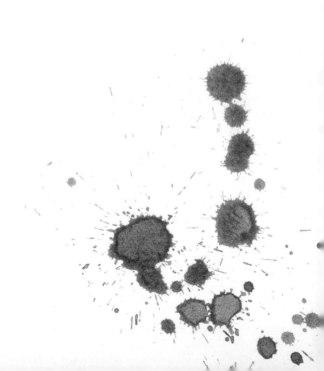

The List

ideas to help rescue the plonker down the well

A Prune

① Rocks (by Bunion)

• Fill well with rocks

• Put them on top of each other

• Climb up.

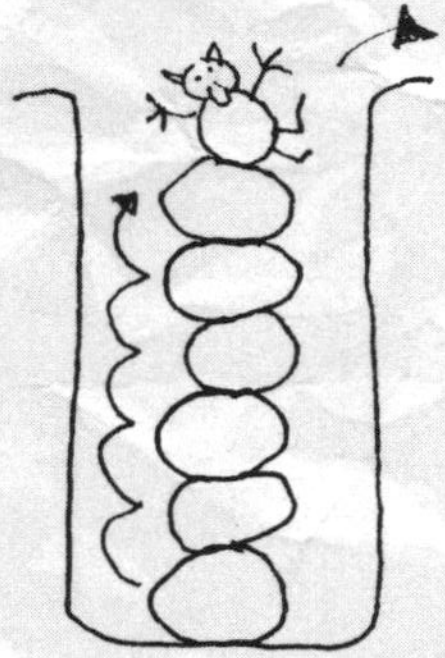

② Prunes (by Teabag)

• To eat if he gets hungry on the way up.

A ← Carrot

③ Carrots (by Fetid)
• To eat if he falls and gets hungry on the way down.

④ Water (by Bunion)
• Fill well with water
• Float to top
• Climb Out

⑤ More Rocks (by Bunion)
• Because I'm Team Leader and my ideas are best.

Bunion sighed again and looked around him. They had just dumped a bunch of carrots down the well but, truthfully, their hearts weren't in it any more.

He tried to think positively. "Why don't we skip number 4 and move straight on to number 5?" he said brightly. "Get some more rocks – right good big ones this time, eh?" He looked around him, smiling. "What do you reckon?"

More Vegetables Please

J ust then, quite unexpectedly, a small voice came quivering up out of the darkness. The Puddle Goblins peered into the well.

"NO MORE ROCKS PLEASE – *RIBBIT* – BUT A COUPLE OF PRUNES WOULD BE NICE – OH YES, AND SOME MORE OF THOSE ORANGEY STICKS – *RIBBIT!*"

"Who's there?" said Teabag, looking up at the sky.

"What's wrong with rocks?" muttered Bunion. "Perfect solution to a very complex problem."

"Well, if it weren't for the carrots he wouldn't know which way was up," growled Fetid.

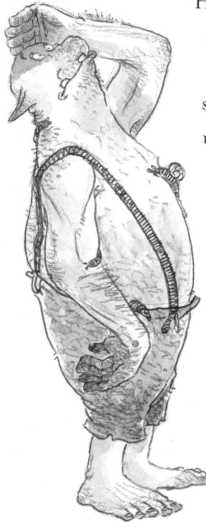

"Help you to see in the
dark, carrots."

"I like prunes,"
said Teabag slowly,
more to himself than
anybody.

The mental strain
of the day was
beginning to show.
The words wobbled
when he spoke,
like a weak battery.
"Dey-feels nice-
and squeezy-when-I
... um, you know
... squeeeeeze
them."

Septic had not liked the rocks. Bit dry and heavy on the stomach. The chewing was particularly difficult. No, stones were just no good – give me knotted slugs and worm-tails any day, he thought*.

But he was better pleased with the prunes and carrots. And of course, he shared everything with Ribbit and Tincup.

"Ribbit," said Ribbit.

"Yes, really quite tasty," agreed Septic. "And your thoughts, Tincup?"

The usual silence. Septic nodded. If Tincup didn't want to talk, that was fine by him – he respected that.

---

* Knotted slugs and worm-tails were just another way to pass the time between meals. It also reminded Septic of his old mum, who always encouraged him to play with his food.

To share silence with a friend and be comfortable was a very special gift. And the one thing that Septic and the bucket spent most of their time doing was sharing lots and *lots* of comfortable silences.

Chapter Fourteen

The Argument

Meanwhile, up top, a fight had broken out and all three Puddle Goblins were biting, pinching and scratching. They were arguing about why Septic had asked for more vegetables and not rocks.

"Because vegetables are good for making windy-pops and rocks are not," Fetid explained.

Bunion felt he was going to lose this argument and wanted to bite someone – preferably a vegetable-eating plonker like Fetid.

"Hang on a minute!" said Teabag. "Can't you hear something?" He was looking up at the sky again.

"That's Septic," said Fetid. "I think we should hear what he's got to say."

"Oh, I see, let's all talk to a plonk what falls down some great big hole in the ground, shall we?" snarled Bunion, who had a good hold of an ankle and was about to give it a bite. He was fed up with being leader.

"Prunes!" cooed Teabag.

"I'll prune *you* in a second," said Bunion.

"Can't you plonkers keep quiet for just one minute?" snapped Fetid.

They all dropped each other and de-tangled themselves. Teabag shuffled forward and, leaning so far into the well it looked like he was going to topple in, he boomed, "COOEEEEE! MR SEPTIC, I'VE ONLY GOT ONE PRUNE LEFT BUT I'M GONNA SEND IT TO YOU RIGHT NOW – OK?"

"Honestly, that plonker has less inside that head of his than a lump of green cheese," mumbled Bunion.

"Oi – did you hear what he called you?" said Fetid. "A plonker!"

"Right! – That's it!" snorted Bunion, his temper finally snapping like a dry twig. He stuffed both hands deep into his pockets, searching angrily for something, anything, to throw at Fetid. Finding nothing better, he picked up a stone and flung it.

It bounced off Fetid's head and landed at Teabag's feet. He saw it and smiled, his yellow teeth seeing daylight for the first time that day.

"Stoney! There you are!"

But Bunion, in one movement, ground it into the dirt with a twist of his foot.

"There!" he said. "What do you make of *that*?"

Teabag gurgled. He slowly rose to his full height and glared down at Bunion. A voice at the very back of Bunion's head nudged its way to the front and told him he *really* shouldn't have done that.

Teabag took a deep breath and roared. Bunion's hair flew up behind him in waves, like

scribbles from a pen. It still stayed that way when
Teabag ran out of breath.

Bunion turned and ran, treading on Fetid's
foot as he passed. Fetid squealed and they all
chased each other around the well.

Teabag stopped, realising he was never going to catch Bunion. He looked around for something to throw and his eyes settled on the oak tree. He snapped off the longest and heaviest branch he could manage and hurled it at Bunion.

It missed. It missed by so much that all three goblins had time to put their hands in pockets and watch the branch fly by in slow motion, continuing its lazy arc until finally disappearing down the well!

"Whoopsy!" said Fetid quietly.

"**Plonk!**" snapped Bunion.

"Stoney!" sniffed Teabag.

All the while, Gooey and Gloop had stayed out of sight, watching in disbelief at just what utter plonkers Puddle Goblins were. Gooey shook her head. "What are they doing? It must be sss-some kind of sss-ceremony to the great hole in the ground!"

"What we need-sss to do," said Gloop, "is get down into that hole. They've been talking to it all day. And feeding it carrots and prunes and stones and stuff."

"You're right, brother of mine," hissed Gooey, her sharp yellow eyes dancing. "We've got to go down it and find out its secrets-sss!"

"Yes-sss! No more sss-stinky sss-smelly fishes-sss!"

Shivering with excitement, they slunk out from under the brambles and oozed their way towards the well.

Septic Sees the Light

"Oh, so very well done," screamed Bunion, his eyes wild. All three were staring at the branch poking out the top of the well. "You slug-infested worm-faced ... *prune!*" (It's all he could think of.) "It's a wonder you know how to put your pants on every morning!"

"Ah, now," began Teabag. "That's not really true. You see, my mum always likes to ..."

"SHUT UP! Don't you understand, you've just killed Septic! He'll be lying down there like a blob of strawberry jam!"

All three Puddle Goblins looked at their feet.

81

But once again, Septic and his friends had
been lucky.

Many, many things had fallen down the well
since Septic had been there. Some were eaten,
some were adopted and some were buried in the
mud. And as time passed the well had begun to
fill up.

The well had filled up even more with the
helpful articles that Bunion, Fetid and Teabag
had thrown down there. And now the tree had
made it just about full!

Climbing the tree branch that by some miracle had also missed squashing him, Septic was at last aware of a daylight he had all but forgotten. He took a peek over the rim of the well.

He frowned. It had been a while but he was sure he knew a Puddle Goblin when he saw one. But what he saw were more like Water Goblins. He bobbed back down, scratched his head, then took another look. Yep, he thought, definitely Water Goblins. Two of them. And they were creeping and crawling towards him.

Teabag, looking at the branch and the well, realised his mistake. He took firm hold and gave it a yank. To his surprise, swinging from the branch was some bizarre mud-dripping creature. At first he thought it must be the frog-goblin.

But no, it was Septic! He
had his bucket over one arm
and, peering over the rim, a
frog was croaking its happy
little heart out.

It was only then that
everyone caught sight of
the Water Goblins.
With a squeal and a
terrifying hiss, Gooey
and Gloop broke into a
run and dived head first
down the well before anyone
could stop them.

One Out, Two In

Instantly Bunion, Fetid and Teabag
disappeared. Where once they had stood,
there was now a line of three puddles. But Septic
was clearly out of practice. He bent down slowly,
turned the bucket upside down and crawled
underneath, though in truth the bucket only just
fitted over his head. He hugged Ribbit, closed
his eyes and thought dark muddy thoughts.

From the well, shouts and screams of elation
came booming up.

"We've done it, we've done it!" they screamed. "You
can't get us-sss now, so you can't – and we're never moving
out of here now. Never! Not until we gets-sss the secret!"

The very well seemed to wriggle with giggles!

Eventually, Fetid and Bunion peeped out of their puddles to listen to the ranting of Gooey and Gloop.

"What's all that about?" said Fetid.

"Beats me!" shrugged Bunion.

Teabag was the next to emerge, but he was clearly flagging after a very demanding day. "I need to rest my thinking," he said and slowly sank back down.

"Ribbit!" said Septic. It took him a lot longer to come out and when he did he clung on to the bucket like a best friend. Inside came the

echo-ey croaks of a frog drumming out a beat.

To the background chorus of the singing Water Goblins, Septic and the others sat down while he told them his story … the bits he could remember.

"What *I* want to know," mumbled Fetid, leaning towards Bunion, "is why he keeps saying *ribbit*?"

"Septic, or the frog?" asked Bunion.

All's Well that Ends Well!

Puddle Goblins only really get together in twos or threes, so it took quite some time for the word to get around that Septic had been found. Indeed, there were those who didn't even know he'd been missing.

Gooey and Gloop remained down the well for nearly six months, almost the same length of time as Septic. They were so convinced it would only be a matter of time before they would find the secret of puddles there. Finally, however, they climbed out and went home, stiff, muddy and very grumpy. The fish idea would have to do for now.

Septic came to visit the well once more, about two years later. He had decided to travel far, far away. He wanted to make up for lost time – do something exciting! He was travelling with a new friend called Disinfectant. Hand in hand, they bent over the edge of the well.

"… and you just leaned in, you say, and with a whiz and a bump and an oh-dear-what-a-plonk, you stayed down there for six months?"

Septic giggled. "Yes, my dear, I did just that, ribbit, and if it wasn't for Tincup and Ribbit I don't think I would have made it, ribbit."

"You must tell me what you did down there. I mean, you must have been right bored, no?"

Septic smiled. "Oh, I don't know. It's amazing how time passes when you have friends."

They turned and made their way over the hill
to a life only goblins can imagine. Tincup swung
from a stick across Septic's shoulder, glinting in
the pink evening light. Inside, Ribbit was
snoring, if indeed that is what frogs do when they
sleep.

A storm far, far away rumbled its intent. Only,
this time, it was thinking about a cloudful of
tricks to play with some Shadow Goblins.

But that's another story …

Afterword

After reading this story you'll probably never look at another puddle in quite the same way – and for good reason! Puddle Goblins and their twitchy fingers are out there, ready to flick and pinch.

They may seem like silly plonks in this story, but beware on a wet, puddle-riddled morning.

Have you never wondered why your socks are often flecked with mud spots? Or perhaps you feel a sudden sharp little nip around the ankle?

Well, now you know!

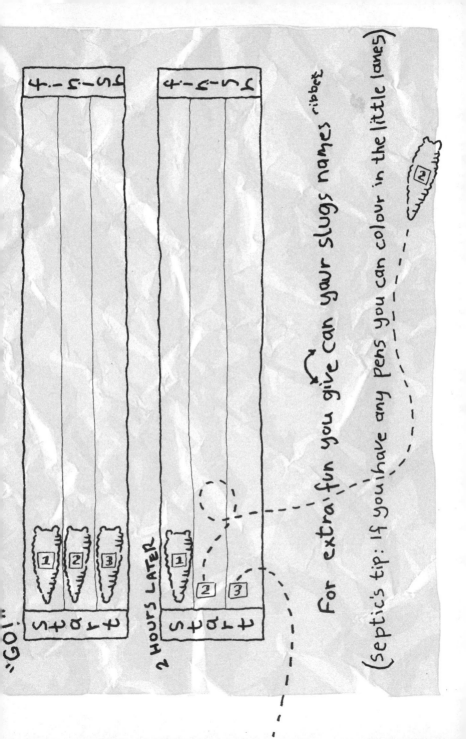

"GO!"

Start

2 HOURS LATER

Start

For extra fun you give can give your slugs names *ribbet*

(septic's tip: if you have any pens you can colour in the little lanes)

Septic's Tips

Things to do if you end up trapped down a hole for six months:

<u>Making new friends:</u>
Make the most of who and what you meet while you're down there. It's amazing how much fun a frog and bucket can be – even if the bucket is a bit moody.

Hug-a-Slug competition:
How many slugs can you hug in three minutes? And, when you've finished, will they all fit in your mouth at the same time? Septic's record is 58.

Blowing saliva bubbles:
Limited entertainment, but hey, it beats counting eye-blinks.

ENJOYED THIS BOOK?

Find out about the other books in the

GOBLINS

series from the website

www.hiddengoblins.co.uk

You can learn about the different characters,
download and print off fun activities
and games, and discover more about
the author, David Melling.

See you there!

stone GOBLINS

tree GOBLINS

puddle GOBLINS

shadow GOBLINS

Can you think of any other kinds of goblin?

David Melling would love to know about your ideas.

Send us a drawing or painting of your goblin, and tell us his or her name.

As well as seeing your picture up on the goblins website, you could win a fantastic goblin goody bag.

We will choose two winners per month.

Send your drawing to:
Goblins Drawing Competition

UK Readers:
Hodder Children's Books
338 Euston Road
London NW1 3BH

Australian Readers:
Hachette Children's Books
Level 17/207 Kent Street
Sydney NSW 2000

New Zealand Readers:
Hachette Livre NZ Ltd
PO Box 100 749
North Shore City 0745

some
goblin
sketches

water Goblin's on the move...

Solitary Gobling

HERMITS, OUTCASTS, LONERS, THE UNSOCIABLE

a goblin appetizer

Burp!

Look out for those
shadow GOBLINS